NORMAN
THE SLUG WITH THE SILLY SHELL

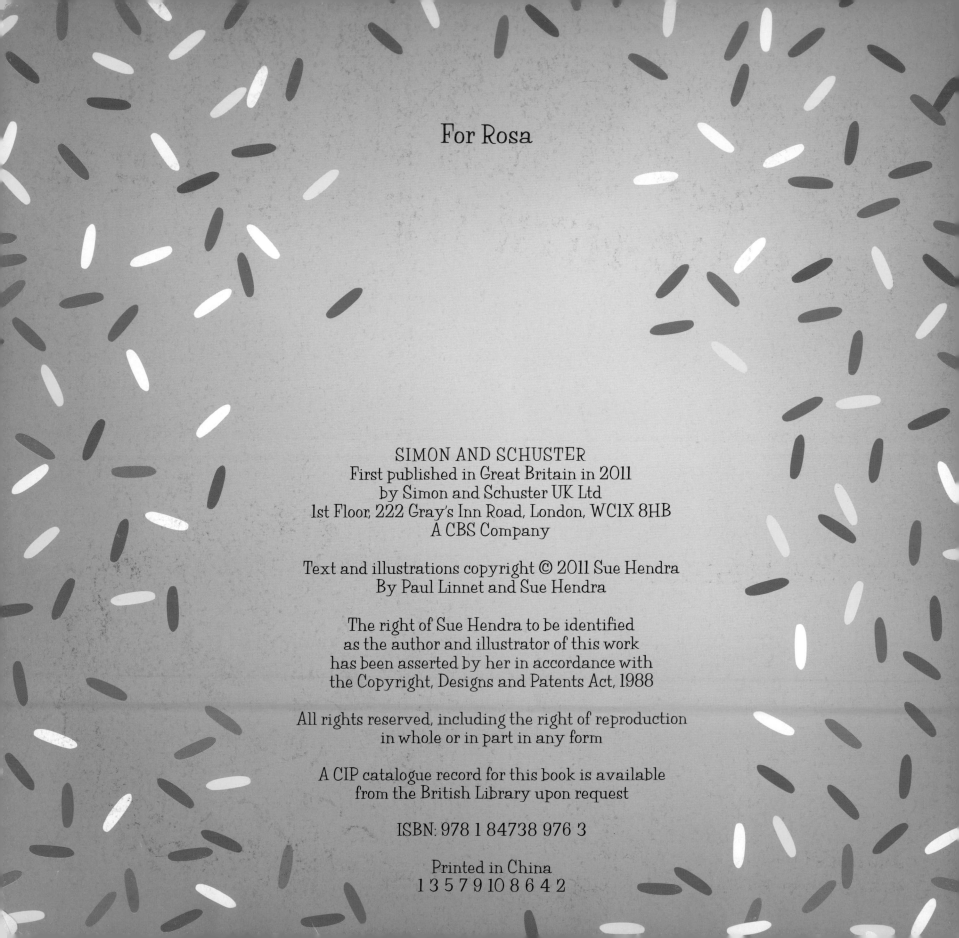

For Rosa

SIMON AND SCHUSTER
First published in Great Britain in 2011
by Simon and Schuster UK Ltd
1st Floor, 222 Gray's Inn Road, London, WC1X 8HB
A CBS Company

Text and illustrations copyright © 2011 Sue Hendra
By Paul Linnet and Sue Hendra

The right of Sue Hendra to be identified
as the author and illustrator of this work
has been asserted by her in accordance with
the Copyright, Designs and Patents Act, 1988

A CIP catalogue record for this book is available
from the British Library upon request

ISBN: 978 1 84738 976 3

Printed in China
1 3 5 7 9 10 8 6 4 2

NORMAN
THE SLUG WITH THE SILLY SHELL

by Sue Hendra

SIMON AND SCHUSTER
London New York Sydney

Norman the slug thought snails were great.
"Wow!" said Norman. "Look at them! They're amazing!"

But, unfortunately, the snails didn't think Norman was great.

WHEE! CRASH!

"Norman, you silly slug!" they cried. "You've spoilt our fun. This only works if you've got a shell."

Norman felt left out. Sadly, he skulked off into the moonlight.

"If only I had a shell of my own," he sighed,
looking at his reflection.

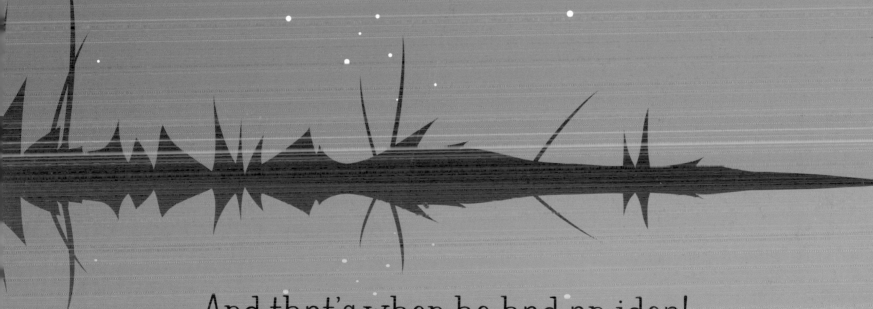

And that's when he had an idea!
"Maybe I could have a shell after all,"
he thought.

But finding a shell was not as easy
as it seemed.

One was too bouncy,

one was too
NOISY,

and one was already taken!

Norman needed time to think . . .

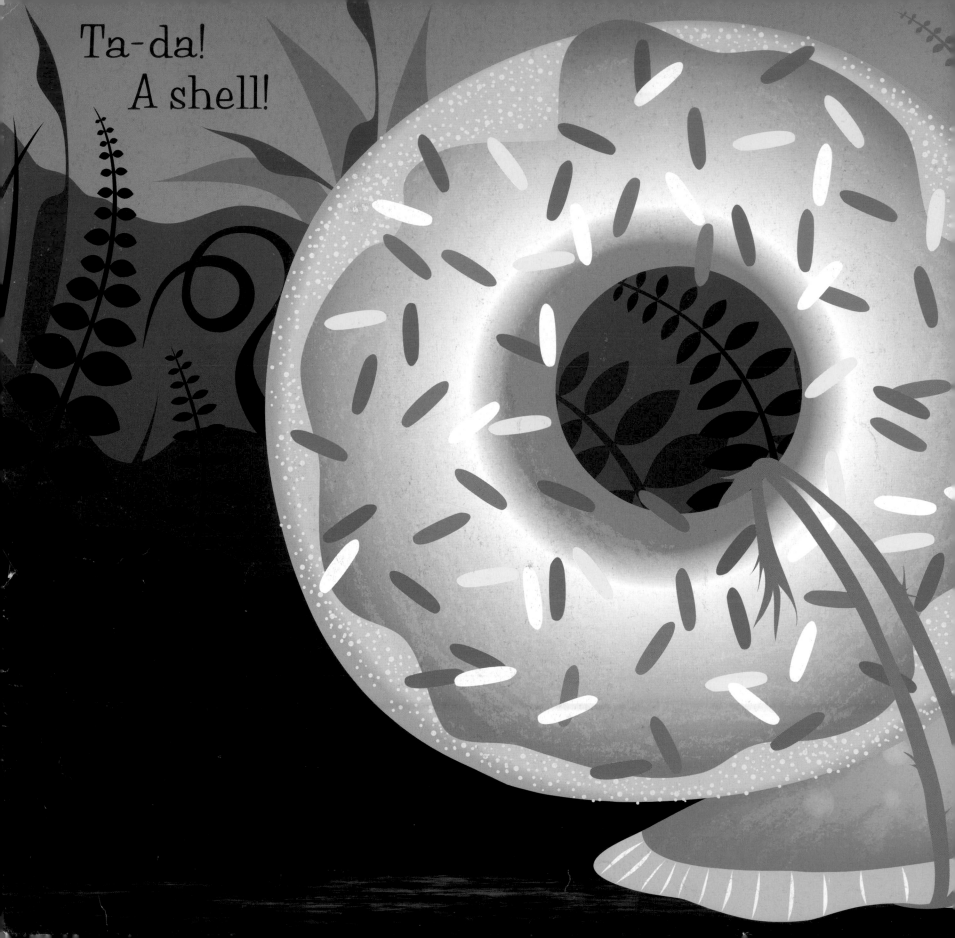

Ta-da!
A shell!

It was perfect!

Norman had never been happier.
He could join the snails at last.

Norman LOVED being a snail.

And the snails LOVED Norman's silly shell.

But the fun didn't last for long.

Suddenly, there was a loud flapping of wings.

"Look out! Bird!" cried the snails in panic.
"Quick, slither for your lives or we'll end up as supper!"

But the bird was more interested in Norman's silly shell – it looked DELICIOUS!

Norman was being carried up, up and away, higher and higher into the sky.

What could he do?

Norman did the only thing a slug could do.
He made slime – lots and lots of it!

With a slither and a slother, a slip and a slide,
Norman was FREE!

But he was falling

faster and

faster and

FASTER until . . .

PLONK!

"Norman, Norman, are you OK?"
asked the snails.

"Wow!" said Norman. "That was great.
I LOVE flying. If only I had wings . . ."

Ta-da!

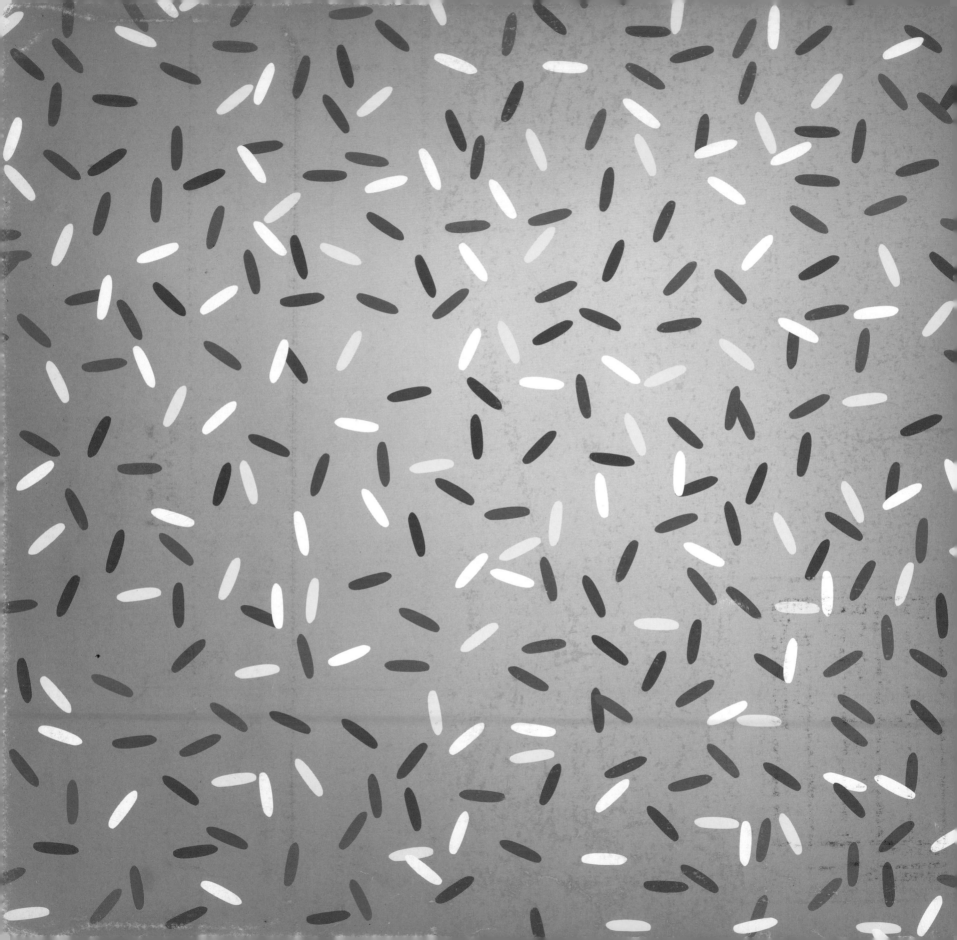